The Diabolical Miracles of Vesturbær

VALERIO GARGIULO

Copyright © 2019 Valerio Gargiulo

ISBN 978-9935-9515-1-9

This book is dedicated to my real friends who, despite the passage of time, remain and do not vanish. I also dedicate it to those who, despite having taken different paths in life, have played an important part in my own spiritual journey.

CONTENTS

ACKNOWLEDGEMENTS

This book was made possible by the many people who inspired and supported me in numerous ways. I am grateful for the support and guidance provided by my daughter Aurora, my parents Ciro and Elvira, my girlfriend Anna, my aunt Adele and my brothers Cristiano and Paolo. I want to thank also Brunella Voto, Manuela Gazzillo, Roberto Cuorvo, Sigurður Pétursson, Dario Farruggia, Cristina Presti, Natasha Dowding, Paul Cota, Marco Perrotta, Silja Pálmarsdóttir, Natasha McKibbin, Gianluca Noci, Joseph Lovecchio, Giuseppe Filodoro and Arndís Björg Sigurgeirsdóttir for their feedback and contributions.

INTRODUCTION

In the previous chapters of the saga, we met Valentino Voto and his dream world. Born and raised in Naples, at some point in his life he decided to drop everything, work, family and friends, to start a new life path.

Its destination is Iceland, an exotic country and light-years away from its Neapolitan culture. Despite the many difficulties encountered, he will be able to complete his doctorate in the pre-Christian mythology of the Scandinavian peoples. He would succeed even if tormented by strange premonitory dreams that will often confuse with reality. On two occasions he will meet an Icelandic girl, the mysterious Gudrun, with whom he eventually falls in love. The events that followed changed his life forever: a series of inexplicable episodes, precognitive dreams, occult and pagan beliefs, elves and other mythical beings, winter night landscapes and northern lights. Is Gudrun really the girl of his dreams or a ghost?

I

I AN EVENING WITHOUT LENA

Garðarshólmi is a mythical and mysterious land. Its landscapes are surreal and magnetic; it almost seems like they want to steal your soul while you are watching.

---

[1] Camille Flammarion, The Atmosphere: Popular Meteorology, 1888.

In this regard, try to make a trip by car along the *Hringvegur*, the only existing highway. You would discover a different reality from that which the man of the 21st century knows, all day connected to the internet, but now disconnected from the frequencies of the transcendental. The first to inhabit it was the Swede Garðar Svavarsson in the 9th century, but according to the Landnámabók ("Book of Settlements"), his discovery was accidental. A storm pushed his boat towards the east coast of the island. After circumnavigating it by mistake, the Viking landed at Skjálfandi (also known as Skjálfandaflói) where he stayed for the whole winter. Returning to his homeland, he informed everyone of its existence and called it after his name. I love *Garðarshólmi* from the bottom of my heart. Perhaps its magical landscapes stole my soul that first time I landed at Keflavík airport, and as a result, it became one with its seductive nature, so alive and unspoiled.

Once an elf told me that Iceland is the last bastion to defend the *Huldufólk*, the so-called "Hidden People". The elf was called Snorri. We met near his home, a large rock located in the park of Hellisgerði, a huge garden full of lava caves, known above all for the many legends about the Hidden People. At that time, I was working as a postman for the fjord agency, and I was waiting for the final contract from the university. Every morning I passed through that garden to deliver letters and advertisements to the locals. There were a few houses around, while everything else was nothing but a huge lava desert. At one point on the tree-lined path, I came across Snorri at random. He was there, a few steps away and he said to me with a worried tone:

"You see, it is not easy to protect a secret nowadays, humans do everything to destroy our wonderful world. They are selfish. They should think more about the nature around us, respect it and protect it for future generations. You are different, Valentino. I know that well."

I was not dreaming, nor imagining who knows which fictional characters. From an early age, on the other hand, I happened to dream with open eyes, but that day was different. I clearly remember his physical appearance and the brief chat made in Hafnarfjörður. He was short and had pointed ears. His eyes were peculiar: they were green, but of intense colours, like those of a wild wolf. This may prove difficult to believe, but the elderly, especially those living in rural areas, still believe in the existence of elves and ghosts. Young people, on the other hand, are not interested in these topics; they consider them a mere figment of the imagination of their ancestors. It must be said, however, that Scandinavia was the last European region to convert to Christianity. He was also the least inclined to accept the new monotheistic cult. In fact, the belief in the Norse gods, such as Odin, Frigg, Thor, Baldr, and Týr, was not immediately abandoned.

The Church thought well of boycotting these primitive beliefs and spread among the Germanic peoples the idea that Odin and the other gods of Norse mythology were diabolical or malign entities. Consequently, these deities were eventually replaced with Christian figures, considered by the people now converted to the new religion, more benevolent and positive than the Pagan gods. Though believing in the supernatural, I still consider myself a good Christian, or at least a spiritual person. Father Santoro, my mentor, would have called me a "rosewater Catholic", which means not a strong faith according to his religious standards. I grew up in a typical Catholic family; my mother tried to keep me away from superstition and the occult. However, Pagan beliefs had always fascinated me. During my university studies, I did numerous anthropological researches on the paranormal and for this reason, I considered myself an expert on the subject.

Professor Jón Magnússon, internationally renowned anthropologist and tutor of my doctoral thesis, had entrusted me at the beginning of last year with a course on the Christianization of Scandinavia. That September evening, Marco picked me up around 6:00 pm. I had just finished the lesson at the Faculty of Social and Cultural Anthropology at the University of Iceland.

"*Ciao*, Valentino, how are you?"

"Well, well. How are you doing? Is your head still aching?" I asked, remembering that a few days before he had been to the doctor for a check-up.

"Every now and then I have strong headaches due, I believe, to the stress accumulated over the past few months. But nothing serious. The doctor prescribed me a supplement based on *Passiflora, Rhodiola Rosea,* and *Ashwagandha.*"

"Ashwa what?" I asked, foolishly amused by the exotic name.

"Just forget it. ..."

My friend looked different to usual as if something inside him had suddenly started boiling like a geyser. He had recently been hired by a bioengineering company, specializing in the design and manufacture of prostheses for people with amputated lower limbs. At first, his Icelandic life was difficult. However, after a period of adaptation and sacrifices, during which he had delivered newspapers and advertisements door-to-door to be rounded up at the end of the month, he finally managed to find that important job to which he aspired. Despite the bad mood expressed that evening, he confided to me that he now felt satisfied and full of expectations for the future. "Valentino, it's gratifying you know, the work I'm doing at LISSIR hf. My supervisor would like to entrust me with new projects," he said in a hoarse voice from agitation.

I looked at him for a moment and gave a smile. But I didn't believe him. There was no enthusiasm in his eyes; his eyes were dull.

Marco Oddur born of an Icelandic mother and spoke the local language correctly, so he did not encounter the same environmental difficulties as his girlfriend. The young woman was called Lena Piotrowska (daughter of Piotr and Dagmara) and was of Polish origin. Although she had earned a master's degree in international law at a prestigious university in Reykjavík, she worked enthusiastically at a municipal nursery. On the other hand, she loved children, and perhaps for this reason too, she liked the job as a teacher. Her family had moved to Iceland from Gdańsk in the late nineties. Gdansk is the city of Lech Wałęsa, the founder of *Solidarność*, the Independent Self-governing Trade Union "Solidarity". Its creation constituted a fundamental event in the history not only of Poland but of the entire communist bloc. Indeed, the advent of the trade union opened a climate of hope and confidence in the new governments in Poland and the rest of Eastern Europe.

The girl was five years old at the time and spoke a clean, correct Icelandic, with a hint of a foreign accent. She was proud of her origins and found it very difficult to build stable friendships. On weekends, she taught the Icelandic language to the children of immigrants at Landakotskirkja's Oratory. Lena often attended our reunions, but this time she did not take part. Marco explained to me that she was tired and preferred to watch the last episode of a television series. We spent the rest of the evening together. Our destination was a club in downtown, where we had been some time ago with other friends. He ordered a huge sandwich with double burgers and two slices of bacon, I chose the vegetarian option which consisted of a Vegan Lentil Meatloaf served with salad. Sitting around an oval table, we began to chat about this and that, until Marco wanted to remember the inexplicable events that occurred in his home in Suðurgata in front of a mug of craft beer.

There are facts that should not be told in public because we would risk our credibility, or worse, appear crazy. Since I don't even like to pass by a braggart, I decided, in agreement with Marco, not to share our bizarre experience with anyone. It was our secret, but I would never forget what we had experienced that day.

"Two years have passed by now. Do you remember?"

"Of course I remember. If I think about it, I still get goose bumps!"

"And yet it seemed completely real."

"For me it certainly was. Only that having interacted with an ectoplasm makes me feel uncomfortable."

To my amazement, it was a ghost; the spectre of a young Icelandic girl. Among other things, this was not the first time I saw her. The first meeting was in Naples in the street, and the second one in Reykjavík that day with Marco. Unfortunately, I did not know her identity and who she really was in a past life. Besides that, I ignored the reason for our encounters. Her name was Gudrun.

I was sure, however, that her appearances were part of paranormal phenomena; that is of events that transcended the normal understanding of reality. I would have liked to have seen her again to ask her a specific question: what was the link between her and I?

"Since I moved to my grandmother's house, nothing unusual has ever happened to me. Lena and I are very well there. My grandmother Solveig decided not to sell it anymore before she died."

"I'm sorry your grandmother died, she was a fantastic woman. But what do you do with that huge garden?"

"Don't talk about it. It's a good thing there is Aunt Birna. She often comes to take care of it. I wouldn't know what to do without her help."

"I think maybe we purified the environment that night. You and I are fantastic Ghostbusters, aren't we?" I commented, tearing a smile from him.

"Sure," Marco winked.

That topic had been a real taboo for almost two years. Lena knew nothing about it. Marco preferred not to tell her anything to keep her from being scared.

The couple apparently lived happily and in harmony in that huge villa. At one point in the evening, a well-dressed and intellectual-looking man approached our table. He must have been around 60/65 years old. He was tall and had a lean body for the age he showed. I thought that perhaps in his free time he devoted himself intensively to caring for his body. He wore a tiny brooch with the logo of the local masonry, called *Frímúrarareglan á Íslandi,* whose motto was the Latin phrase *sub specie aeternitatis,* which literally means "under the aspect of eternity". This expression, used in Christian theology, indicated the way to consider events under a universal profile, that is, regardless of any consideration of time and place. The case had wanted me to talk about it recently to my students during a lecture on Icelandic corporations and Christianity. The local lodges required their members to be Christian practitioners and specifically to profess the Lutheran rite, thus demonstrating they were strongly indoctrinated.

"Guys, excuse the intrusiveness. Can I sit down?"

The man knew our language. This was something I did not expect and caught me off guard. On the contrary, the fact that he wanted to sit with us hadn't surprised me that much. During the weekend it was not uncommon to see such scenes. Often the "autochthonous" go to the pubs in the centre alone and after drinking too many beers, they change their suspicious attitude becoming magically more sociable. There were a few moments of indecision, then I invited him to sit.

"My name is Sigurður Bjarni Baldursson, but my friends call me just Siggi. I heard your conversation and I knew you were Italian. I have a small farmhouse near Figline Valdarno. I go there when I can with my wife Flora. Like me, she loves Italy. We have a Norwegian friend who lives all year in Tuscany with whom we share a passion for gardening. Now she is taking care of it in our absence. You should see our beautiful aubergines that grow in our little garden."

Siggi spoke about himself for a whole hour without stopping. He told us he was a judge at Reykjavík District Court, and he owned two German shepherds and four Icelandic horses, a breed similar to ponies. As I suspected at the beginning, he admitted being a Freemason and belonging to the Grand Lodge of Selfoss.

"I have been elected Grand Master for a few months, so I am the highest member in the hierarchy of my Lodge," he stated proudly.

Realizing that he had monopolized the conversation, he tried to remedy it by asking us some questions.

"Guys, pardon me if I have spoken all the time. I have to admit that sometimes I talk too much. What are you doing in Iceland? Have you come to see the Northern Lights by chance?"

"No problem. It was very interesting what you were telling us," Marco answered sarcastically yawning on purpose, but Siggi paid no attention to his rude gesture.

"My name is Valentino and I was born in Naples. I teach Social and Cultural Anthropology at the University of Iceland. I recently published a thesis on the pre-Christian myths of the Scandinavian peoples, even though I recently started a new study on the history of Christianity in Iceland and on how it has influenced Pagan cults of the past."

"Interesting. And tell me, don't you miss Italy? Our winters are extremely cold, and it seems absurd to me that a Neapolitan wants to live here," he argued, emphasizing a certain astonishment.

"Living in Naples was starting to be tight and for this reason, I moved to Reykjavík."

"I understand you very well. *Heimskt er heimaalið barn.*"

"What does it mean?" I asked, not grasping the meaning of this Icelandic sentence.

"It means that a child needs to leave home to learn," Marco answered, anticipating Siggi's reply.

"Exactly! I bet you learned Icelandic to conquer a girl who did not love you back. Am I right?"

It was an unfortunate joke that motivated Marco to be even ruder.

"What nonsense. My mother is an Icelander, and my father is Italian. What else do you want to know?"

Siggi was a bit tipsy but he seemed like a good person and I was sorry that Marco was treating him in such an arrogant and unfriendly way.

"I was pleased to meet you. This is my business card. Let's meet for coffee, Valentino. I would like to learn more about your academic studies."

"My pleasure, Siggi. Whenever you want."

"See you soon, then, and have a good time."

Perhaps the judge felt like an intruder on a very private moment and he politely left us alone. Siggi rose from his chair and disappeared into thin air from our view. He was certainly a gentleman, but also a great talker.

"This man believed he knew everything," Marco commented contemptuously," it was clear that he was trying to impress us with those stories about his life and his career."

"To me, on the other hand, he seemed a cultured and distinguished person. He was certainly talkative but not a liar."

While I enjoyed tracing Siggi's psychological profile and analysing the reliability of what he had just told us, Marco received a phone call. We thought it was Lena since she was home waiting for him. The line was disturbed and the number did not appear on the smartphone display.

"How strange. I have never received an anonymous call since moving to Iceland," Marco said in some perplexity.

We resumed our conversation, not caring too much about that episode. Another ten minutes passed, then another unanswered call. We counted five in total, until Marco, unnerved by all those phone calls, decided to contact Lena to check if everything was okay. Unfortunately, his girlfriend did not reply. The situation was degenerating, and Marco's concern increased exponentially.

He started to get up, and then he sat down again. His behaviour was hysterical, but I could do nothing but calm him down.

"She'll be sleeping at this hour, that's why she doesn't answer you," I stated, trying to minimize his worries.

"I'm afraid something bad happened to her. That's why she doesn't answer me."

"Come on, Marco."

His apprehension seemed excessive and I pointed this out to him, but it was all in vain. Marco was too tense to listen to me.

"Hurry up, I'll give you a ride," he said, regardless of my assurances.

It was like talking to a deaf man. Marco was no longer listening to me. He had drunk at least three beers in that club, and perhaps it was not the best idea to accept his invitation to take me back. Regardless, I decided to go with him. It was raining heavily outside and I wanted to avoid getting a cold again. My apartment was in Vesturbær, a neighbourhood located west of the historic centre of Reykjavík.

It was the first district to develop when the Icelandic capital was only a small village. The actual growth occurred at the end of the 19th century when the city became the intellectual centre of the island. When we arrived outside my apartment building entrance, the digital clock display on the dashboard of his Fiat 500 showed two in the morning.

"Good night, Marco."

Marco didn't answer.

"*Ue*, good night!" I repeated with more determination, waiting for his greeting.

Nothing to do. He looked at me with a crazy expression that worried me. Then I left the cockpit and watched him for a few moments from the door of the building where I live. He set off again at full speed and even risked investing a boy who was walking down the street. I had never seen anything like it. It was as if Marco was under the influence of drugs, or worse as if an alien or an evil entity had taken possession of his mortal body.

"Let's hope not," I said to myself.

Exhausted, I took refuge at home. I wore the brightly coloured pyjamas that my aunt Simona had given me for a birthday, and I immediately went to bed to rest. Tired as I was at the end of that intense evening, I instantly fell asleep. The next day would be a long day.

2

2 A BAD OMEN

The room was dark and silent, there was only the sound of
rain falling inexorably outside to interrupt the tranquillity
of the neighbourhood.

---

[2] Salvator Rosa, The Dream of Aeneas, 1663.

Despite the quiet of Reykjavík at that time of night, I suddenly awoke from sleep. A nightmare had scared me to death. I had the unsettling feeling that it was a premonition. I breathed deeply to relax, but it wasn't enough. I slipped from the bed with extreme caution, like a thief trying to avoid triggering the alarm of a bank he is about to rob. Without messing up the sheets and the linen blanket that my mother had sent me from Naples, I went directly to the bathroom to calm down. I looked fearfully in the mirror in the way a teenager would notice unwanted pimples on his face. Everything was in order. I closed the bathroom door and went to the kitchen. From the jug resting on a shelf, I poured water into a glass that I don't think I had ever drunk. As I returned to my bedroom quite alarmed, I took the dream diary from the nightstand drawer. I considered the dream activity a mystical and contemplative experience not to be underestimated in terms of useful information to decode; that's why I used to write in a journal what I could still remember and visualize when I woke up.

The idea came to me reading an article from an Italian newspaper on the famous film director and screenwriter Federico Fellini, one of the few filmmakers I saw all his movies. He too had this curious custom; in fact, many of his scripts were inspired by dreams. I particularly remembered the script of one of his films that remained unfinished, I had found it fascinating and mysterious: *Il Viaggio di G. Mastorna, detto Fernet.* Several times Fellini tried to realize it, but a series of setbacks and nefarious events continually hindered its realization. His friend Gustavo Rol, a great spiritual master, strongly advised against going ahead with that project. Given the meaning that the director gave to dreams and certain ominous omens, the film and script were never completed. As far as I am concerned, the diary had on several occasions proved to be a useful tool for remembering the details of my dreams to which I later gave hidden and premonitory meanings. However, it was also a way to express and relieve the emotional tensions accumulated during the day.

I wrote down everything I could remember, filling the pages even with little drawings to better fix the memories. Here is what I was able to write and display on my notes.

Out of the corner of my eye, I saw Marco and Lena in a place I didn't know. The room was not furnished, except for the chairs and table where the couple were chatting carelessly. I stood by a fire and watched my friends curiously from afar. They were beautiful and I was sure they were genuinely in love.

Suddenly, it began to rain, only we were inside an indoor salon. We were wet despite being inside that room. The rain came from the ceiling; there were thunder and lightning that threatened us from above.

In the next room, I saw a skeletal man who was tormented by three little demons. Instead from the window, I saw three men running and shouting like they had been possessed by the devil.

I noticed two other skeletal men hanging upside down on a protruding beam.

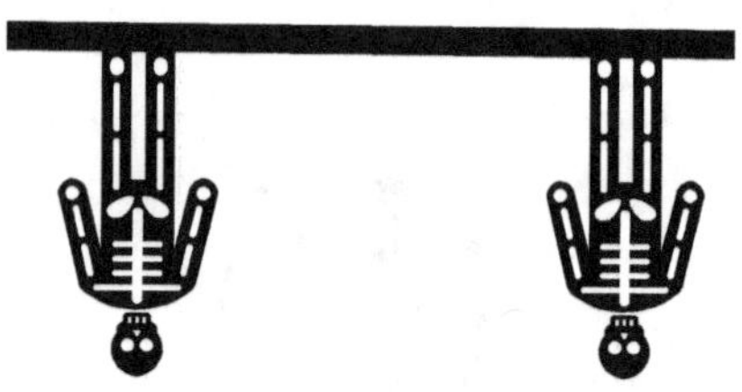

All this worried me. Marco and Lena were still sitting; but now they were arguing, regardless of the internal rain and the screams that came from outside.

"We have to leave. Hurry up! Come this way," said Marco, alarmed. Something or someone had disturbed them.

"Where should we go?" Lena asked absently.

"To hell!" Replied a strong, resonant voice.

It was at that precise moment that I regained consciousness and started to behave like a madman within my house. I had the senseless certainty that something terrible was about to happen. Perhaps I was raving in delirium, lost in the depths of the absurdity of my thoughts: that nightmare seemed to be a clear alarm. But what exactly was going to happen? Any attempt to go back to sleep turned out to be pointless. I saw no other solution than to pray and ask for the protection of Gerard Majella, my guiding spirit and a saint by the Catholic Church. Gerard and I met at the right time. I was in Naples and I was leaving for Iceland and as I was walking out of my building to reach my father Antonio's car, I found a prayer card of him on the street. Holy cards are small, devotional pictures mass-produced for the use of the faithful, and popular collectible items. Majella's card was dirty and even stained with coffee, wrinkled and soaked. It seemed, at first sight, something of little account but despite this, I found it special. I picked it up and put it in my pocket.

I considered that finding as a divine sign; an extraordinary event from which I could draw clues, deductions and new knowledge. I was thrilled to have received that gift. Hence, I decided in an irrational (but I don't think arbitrary) way to name Gerard my guardian angel. From that day in fact, I turn to him when I need his help. I am very happy with Saint Gerard Majella; the prayers of protection that I address to him when I find myself in difficulty almost always work. When they do not work, I understand that his assistance is not necessary, as it would be fundamental lessons that need to be learned without looking for "angelic shortcuts". In those cases, you can't cheat. In fact, certain difficulties encountered during earthly life are indispensable for the success of each one of us. The morning came as liberation and I had no desire to stay in my room and think about the night. I needed to distract myself and go outside to get fresh air.

I opened the kitchen window and looked out into the street. It was a cold autumn day. The snow, therefore, had not yet made its appearance in the city. At that time on a Sunday, there was no one around, except for an elderly gentleman with his dog, a splendid specimen of Dalmatian with large black eyes. Everything seemed normal, all things considered, but not for me, who continued to feel shaken by that nightmare. Something bad could have happened. This was my concern. I had a quick breakfast of AB-mjólk - a delicious Icelandic yogurt - and then decided to go and have a cappuccino in my favourite café. The bar-library was called Stúdiókaffi and was located in an old building right downtown. I loved that place. It was there that I first heard about diabolical miracles from an Argentine Jesuit priest whom I met that day. Our meeting was completely unexpected. The cafeteria was already full of American and European tourists from the nearby hotel. It was mostly travellers looking for breath-taking scenery.

After a long wait and a gruelling search among the busy tables, I finally found a place next to an arched window. The Jesuit had placed his large cloth bag on a windowsill. My table was near the same windowsill. He was sitting on a padded chair and staring at something outside when he turned. Noticing my presence, he spoke to me.

"Coffee is an exceptional drink. Its aroma would put anyone in a good mood, even that grumpy devil named Beelzebub, who gets angry easily," he said, amused.

He kept talking without introducing himself and told me an anecdote about the origins of coffee.

"An Ethiopian legend tells that a shepherd named Kaldi would have been its discoverer. One day his goats chewed the leaves of the plant and will stay awake and lively until late at night. Observing their anomalous behaviour, Kaldi guessed that they had eaten the seeds of the plant and came up with the idea of toasting them.

He obtained an infusion of black colour, and that was the first coffee of history."

The priest was a charismatic and mysterious character. His face was full and soft. The eyes were of intense dark colour, almost hypnotic. His hair was thick and raven, just like his big eyebrows. Although he was not particularly tall, his bearing was as majestic as that of a Teutonic knight. He must have been around 40-45 years old. After sweetening his double espresso, he finally introduced himself.

"I am Father Ramón Vasquez Vicario, on a special mission on behalf of the Roman Curia," he announced with a smile that gave him confidence.

"On a special mission? Can I know what it is about if I'm not being too intrusive?" I asked curiously.

"Are you able to keep a secret, if I tell you one?"

I didn't know if he was joking or not, but in the end, in uncertainty, I made an affirmative gesture with my head.

"In addition to being priest, I am also an instructor. In my courses, I teach lay people to recognize diabolical possessions and miracles. There is a growing spread in the Scandinavian countries and in the rest of Europe of occultism and Satanism."

I was stunned. I seemed to experience a déjà-vu. I thought back to the nightmare of last night and I looked for a logical connection between improbable premonitions and simple fantasies. Then my turn came and I presented myself to the priest.

"My name is Valentino and I teach Cultural Anthropology at the University of Iceland. Actually, I had never heard of diabolical miracles, even though I am a great scholar of occultism and an expert on Pagan religions."

At that point, Father Ramón retook the floor.

"The Bible warns us and tells us that the Diavolo can disguise himself as an angel of light and can perform miracles of any kind."

Our conversation lasted more than an hour. In my heart, I was happy to have made his acquaintance and to have found a new friend to talk about such subjects.

As I listened to him, I realized that I had forgotten the phone in Marco's car the night before. I made up my mind and remembered that I had placed it on the dashboard. I was sure I would find it there again.

"Now excuse me but I have to go. I think I left my phone in a friend's car and would like to retrieve it."

"Go ahead. I was pleased to converse with you. I write you my e-mail and the mobile number on this sheet. I am sure we will meet soon."

"Certainly. This is my business card. I too was pleased, Father."

"Let's stay in touch, then. May God bless you, Valentino!"

3

3 MANDRAGORA AUTUMNALIS

I left the cafeteria and accelerated my pace. It would take me between ten and fifteen minutes to reach Suðurgata's villa.

---

³ Hieronymus Brunschwig, *Kleines Destillierbuch*, 1500.

I knew the path off by heart. From my starting position, I turned left and I found myself in Vesturgata, a street located in the western part of the city centre. Most of its buildings are residential but there are also some commercial and tourist activities that characterized the whole area. Then I came into a new street, named Aðalstræti, the oldest and perhaps the most famous street in Reykjavík. In fact, the ruins of a Viking-age hut, dating back to the years 868-874, were found here in a basement. When I arrived in Túngata, I made an unusual discovery. I noticed on the ground, in the grass, some leaves of *Mandragora officinarum*; as it is native to regions around the Mediterranean Sea, it seemed to me unusual to see it during the Icelandic autumn. Furthermore, it is a very rare plant organism even in its natural habitat. According to numerous medieval legends, the mandrake was one of the main ingredients for the preparation of various magic potions; because it contains deliriant hallucinogenic tropane alkaloids and the shape of its roots often resembles human figures, it had been associated with a variety of superstitious practices throughout history.

Full of wonder and surprise, I continued my walk towards Marco's home. The closer I got to the villa, the more a sense of anguish increased within me. In the short path between Túngata and Suðurgata, a thousand thoughts came to my mind from which I could not free myself. Inexplicably I could not control myself and I was constantly losing my temper. The priest's words about diabolical miracles began to ring again into my brain. I immediately thought back to the nightmare that had terrified me the night before. It was like an emotional storm. I took deep breaths and I tried to justify myself with losing control. The events that followed, occurred with such rapidity that it was difficult to accept them. Despite the shock they caused me, I was able to visualize and order them according to a chronological scheme. Five Icelandic police cars - with the Lögreglan logo on the rear doors - were outside the gate of Marco's villa with lights flashing. An ambulance had the engine running, it was probably waiting for someone to be transported to the local hospital or at worst its morgue.

The front door was wide open as if it had become an open-pit. A small crowd of onlookers were kept at bay by strips of yellow and black duct tape. A national television crew were preparing to broadcast live for the news. It was obvious that something serious had happened and I started to worry seriously. All that deployment of men did not bode anything good. I tried unsuccessfully to go through the security cordon but there was no way. Frustrated by the failed attempt to ask an agent for more information, I slipped off the corner of a private road and waited, observing the scene that kept updating in front of my astonished eyes. Out of nowhere, a voice said my name and I jumped as if they had awakened me from a nightmare that unfortunately was still in the making.

"Valentino, how lucky to have found you."

I turned around and I saw that the person who was calling me was Marco's maternal aunt.

"They arrested him, they arrested him!" She repeated with desperation.

"Who was arrested?" I asked, already expecting the answer.

Birna was pale and visibly upset. I started to sweat, and that scared me.

"The police arrested Marco. The agents didn't tell me much, only that they took him to Litla-Hraun prison."

The plot seemed worthy of a detective novel. I took my notebook and wrote down some notes on the final pages:

1. *A friend ending up in jail;*
2. *An ambulance waiting for someone that's been hurt, or worse, murdered;*
3. *A crowd comprised of onlookers, journalists and Icelandic police gathering outside Marco's villa.*
4. *A hysterical woman (Birna) in panic and despair.*

"Have you already contacted a lawyer?"

In the end, this was the only question that came to my mind.

"Yes, I called Ingi, an old friend of mine from the high-school. He will be here soon with more precise information."

I worried about my friend. The situation worsened when a stretcher with a dead person left the house followed by a large group of policemen, paramedics, and police officers. It seemed obvious to me that somebody had been killed within those walls. I couldn't and didn't want to believe this eventuality, but the facts spoke for themselves.

"And who would be the killer? Marco *minn*? That's impossible and unimaginable," Birna said desperately.

Marco had been arrested and this suggested that he was at least one of the suspects. In this regard, I was reminded of a phrase by Lucio Anneo Seneca, the famous Roman philosopher and politician, exponent of eclectic stoicism of the imperial age:

"Crimes can go unpunished, but they cannot leave in peace those who committed them."

Certainly, Birna and I, although unrelated to the crime committed, were not at all in peace. Indeed, we were both lost and alarmed by the fate of both Marco and Lena. A dark-glassed BMW slowly approached the sidewalk and to my amazement, I recognized the guy we met in the pub the night before among the crew on board. Birna had listened to the conversation between some policemen next to her who said that the man was a judge in the Reykjavík district court. By a curious coincidence, the magistrate in charge of the preliminary investigations was precisely Siggi - the lover of Italy and Tuscany. I didn't waste time and tried to get noticed. When he was close to me, I made an eloquent sign with my hand, and he recognized me. Despite that, Siggi did not stop, rather he quickened his step towards the entrance of the villa. So, I tried to get closer. This time the attempt was successful, although I managed to speak to him just for a few seconds.

"Siggi, wait a minute!"

"Valentino, I'm sorry but this is not the right place to talk. I'm busy."

He did not seem to be the same joker of the previous evening. Surprised by my perseverance, he accepted to meet me later in front of the Embassy of the Russian Federation, which was located in Túngata, the street of many other buildings and diplomatic facilities.

"See you in forty minutes."

I accepted his proposal and confirmed that I would be on time. In the meantime, as anticipated by Birna, the lawyer, Ingi Berg Guðmundsson, the jurist contacted by her, made his appearance. The man seemed worried and somewhat uncomfortable. On closer inspection, I noticed that he was wearing the same pin that Siggi wore the previous evening; in all probability he also belonged to the masonry. In addition to the brooch, there was another gadget that caught my attention. It was a medallion depicting a golden swastika similar to a solar disk, used by the German Workers' Party and the Thule Society.

Seeing that Nazi symbol left me puzzled. The Thule Society was a German esoteric organization characterized by heated nationalism and intense anti-Semitism. Its name was a tribute to the legendary island of Thule believed by the Germanic people as their mythical homeland. Ingi held out his hand and introduced himself. Birna thanked him for coming to help and for offering his legal assistance. After the pleasantries ended, the lawyer confirmed what we already suspected.

"I am sorry to inform you that Marco Oddur has been arrested for the murder of Lena Piotrowska."

There was a moment of silence, then Birna exclaimed aloud:

"My nephew can't be the culprit!"

The woman felt herself failing and leaned against a light pole. She was pale and could barely stand up. On the lawyer's face, however, I seemed to see an expression of compassion for her old friend, tremendously agitated by what had happened.

Birna reacted in some way to the terrible news, and turning to Ingi said:

"I want to nominate Valentino as the person to be informed about anything concerning this case. I am not able to take it to care at the moment. I'm so sorry for my nephew and that poor girl!"

Marco's aunt looked at me and on the verge of tears, asked me to follow up on this matter. I was totally blown away by her proposal. I would have liked to refuse and leave as far as possible. My sixth sense advised me to stay away from that story. But, how could I turn my back on her?

"Okay, as you like. When there are updates, I will definitely contact him," replied the lawyer.

The tragic circumstance and Birna's sprawling reaction to that horrible news did not allow me to say no. I didn't have the courage. However, there was a technical problem that would have prevented me from being reachable. The night before I had forgotten my cell phone in the Fiat 500.

"Yesterday I left my cell phone in Marco's car," I announced, hoping at the last minute to get away with it.

"Please, just keep mine. I have an old one in a drawer at home, but it's still working," she replied, holding out her smartphone.

Nothing to do, I could not get away this time. So, I grudgingly accepted the task. Birna hugged me tightly before going back home. She would notify the sad news to Marco's parents herself as soon as she felt able to do it. Within minutes her little world, made of gardening and chats with friends around the neighbourhood, had collapsed on herself. Ingi offered Birna a ride, but she refused.

"I prefer to walk. I need some fresh air."

"Okay, then. But if you need anything, really anything, count on me and my wife Rós," said the lawyer thoughtfully.

His gesture seemed sincere to me, and I even went so far as to think that in the past there had been a love story between the two old Icelanders.

Before leaving, however, Ingi handed me his business card with all the info needed to track him down. It was time for me to meet the judge in Túngata.

4 SUDDENLY THE DOUBT

The embassy of the Russian Federation was located within a fairly large complex of buildings. The two nations boasted a long friendship, which began in 1926 when Iceland officially recognized the Soviet Union as a state. In addition, Russian scientists have made a great contribution over the years to the study of the island, especially with regard to its geological mapping.

The BMW was on time. Siggi told me to sit in front of the driver, a burly Icelandic, dressed in a black uniform, who opened the door to get me in. As soon as I fastened my seat belt, we left for an unknown destination. In the car, in addition to the judge and his driver, there was another guy who wore civilian clothes and carried a small briefcase with him as if it were something special. The man was very elegant and sported a well-groomed beard. His name was Logi Ragnarsson and he was the chief of police in Reykjavík. He told me about the dramatic phases preceding Marco's arrest.

"About three o'clock tonight, our switchboard received numerous reports from the residents of Suðurgata, alarmed by the shouts coming from your friends' house. We sent our patrol cars on the spot to carry out checks. The agents knocked on the door of the villa several times, but no one answered. As no one opened, they broke the door with a ram. Lena was lying on the floor of the entrance. The poor thing was already dead. Her body had been pierced by eighteen stab wounds in the back. We had never seen anything like this in Iceland."

Siggi interrupted Logi's story and continued it by giving me more details.

"When they entered the salon, they found your friend in a confused state. He kept repeating incomprehensible words and threateningly brandished a bloody knife against the agents; in the end, he was disarmed by one of the policemen present during the raid."

I could hardly believe it, but I was starting to have serious doubts about Marco's innocence. The reality that was being revealed was horrendous and surreal. Questions stirred within me which I could not answer objectively. Could Marco ever have become a ruthless killer overnight? Although I began to suspect him, Lena's murder remained apparently inexplicable to me. For what dark reason would he kill her?

"What time did you and Marco say goodbye last night?" Logi asked, interrupting my narrow thoughts.

"It was at two o'clock, I remember this very well!" I replied firmly.

"Have you not noticed anything different than usual?" The judge urged me, touching my left shoulder from the back seat.

"Actually, he had been acting strangely the whole evening. First of all, he was nervous and unfriendly. Then he made me uncomfortable when we met you in that club. I assure you that normally Marco is a kind and sociable person. I cannot explain his behaviour yesterday."

"Do you remember anything else unusual that you would connect with what happened next?"

"Maybe yes. Marco received a series of unanswered calls that had actually alarmed him a lot. His concern seemed excessive to me. He thought it was Lena and the idea that something bad had happened had made him very anxious. He tried to call her several times, but she didn't answer any of his calls. Despite my constant reassurances, there was no way to reason with him."

"Good. Then we'll do some technical checks with the telephone company to locate the user's number and address," the police chief replied satisfied.

"What time did you say goodbye to Marco?" Siggi asked again.

"As I said, it was two in the morning. But what is that, an interrogation?"

I burst into growing frustration. Straight after, the two men didn't ask me any more questions. The BMW was not traveling at great speed. In spite of that slow movement, we had travelled many kilometres. In addition to the car I was in, another vehicle was following us at a safe distance; I thought I saw the model; maybe it was an Audi A7. For sure we were in an isolated area, far from the city centre. I could see the vastness of the lava desert and glaciers in the distance from the window. The surrounding rocks gave the impression of being alive, almost as if they were waiting to move. The Icelandic volcanic nature had fascinated me from the beginning. Perfect for those who, like me, desired to live in a magical place, where fire and ice were united, creating unique and suggestive landscapes.

Thinking back, the creation of so many legends about the *Huldufólk* could not have been solely the result of the imagination and boredom of the inhabitants of the island. I had personally met an elf, and this direct testimony could refute once and for all my doubts about the existence of the Hidden People. However, I kept wondering why it was extremely difficult to really believe it; to believe in something that would exist on an ethereal level, but not directly perceivable by the five human senses. Sometimes, I think that our reality could be considered as a kind of radio station in the midst of a plurality of other stations and frequencies. Experts in parapsychology and mediumship believe, among other things, that our brain is capable of recording only a minimal percentage of these extrasensory perceptions. Sometimes there would be an interference between these overlapping dimensions, during which such fleeting encounters with elves and other hidden creatures would occur.

"Valentino, we have arrived," said someone inside the car, abruptly interrupting my theories about the Huldufólk.

Unexpectedly we stopped near a large armoured gate; it was the entrance to Litla-Hraun prison, the largest in the country. The other car that was following us was gone from my view. This penitentiary complex was located not far from the village of Eyrarbakki, along the southern coast of the island. Litla-Hraun consisted of nine buildings, protected by a fence system for maximum safety with anti-cut and anti-climb rectangular grids. Although it could look like a sort of Icelandic Alcatraz seen from the outside, detainees were sometimes granted probation and even the possibility of returning home on weekends in case of good conduct.

"Why did you bring me here?" I asked bewildered.

"We want you to meet Marco," Logi replied, patting me on the shoulder.

"We think it's a good idea. Maybe he will explain the reasons for his crazy gesture. We will be in a room listening to you," added Siggi.

Their initiative provoked mixed feelings in me. Marco was still my best friend, as well as the reference point on that distant island. I didn't want to snatch a confession from him. However, if I had refused, I would have regretted not having met him and looked him in the eye. So I accepted by making a counter-proposal to the two Icelanders.

"Okay, but on one condition. If Marco tells me he is innocent, providing precise and coherent alibis, promise me that the investigation will continue in other directions, perhaps acquiring further evidence."

Logi did not reply clearly, but he did not seem contrary to my proposal either. On the contrary, Siggi was more expressive and nodded with a gesture of the head that said yes. After a few seconds, the gate opened with a metallic click.

We left the sedan parked beyond the fence and continued walking to the prison gate. We walked side by side, me, Logi and Siggi, without saying a word, to the armoured door of one of the nine buildings. Apparently, it was the main one, where a warden was waiting for us, wearing curious eyeglasses with a yellow frame.

"*Góðan daginn,*" greeted the jailer.

"*Góðan daginn,*" we replied almost in unison.

This expression literally means 'good day' and is the standard greeting across Iceland. If, on the other hand, you are familiar with the interlocutor, you can use the male *Saell*, or the female *Sael*. The prison guard, after explaining the rules for visitors, took me to a stinky closet (probably a small changing room for guests) where I left my jacket and a bag with my laptop. Straight after the latest recommendations, the warden unlocked a reinforced door that was behind him. He told me to go down a corridor that looked like a bottomless pit as long and spooky as it was.

I hesitated, then I advanced several meters. I was alone; only with myself and with my distressing feelings. I felt like I was entering a place infested with dark, evil entities. I took courage and reached the end of that hellish corridor, where another agent was waiting for me.

"Please, this way. Your visit will last half an hour," he told me.

The quiet of that place immediately impressed me. I thought that perhaps the detainees were sleeping or were engaged in rehabilitation and recreational activities in one of the other buildings of the prison complex. Suddenly, however, a siren activated and broke the surreal silence.

"What is going on?" I asked the agent next to me.

"*Bíddu aðeins*," he said in Icelandic, which means 'wait a minute'.

A dozen policemen came from the corridor that I had just crossed in a hurry and in riot gear. Siggi and Logi followed them visibly concerned.

The situation seemed bizarre to me. The two men looked at each other and said something in Icelandic that I didn't grasp. A few seconds later, Logi received a phone call and stepped back two or three meters.

"Siggi what's going on?"

"I don't know, Valentino. Let's wait for Logi to finish the call."

The police chief spoke on the phone for about twenty minutes. While waiting for more information, I sat down on a bench located in the warden's room when a painting that hung on the wall caught my attention. The image depicted an ancient map of Iceland. I got up to see it up close and noticed a date at bottom right: "Hólmavík, 17 July 1268". Hólmavík is a village in the western part of Iceland, by Steingrímsfjörður. This detail made me think back to the lucid dream I had previously, in which a sect of intellectuals, philosophers and bankers was precisely called the Sorcerers of Hólmavík. It was just another strange coincidence.

In the meantime, Logi had finished the call and immediately updated us:

"Marco tried to commit suicide."

I was dumbfounded.

"But how is this possible? And nobody noticed it?"

"Unfortunately, no. While under interrogation, he tried to cut his throat with a penknife. It seems he is ok."

"Sorry, so why did you let me come here if you knew he was being interrogated?"

"It should have ended before our arrival. We couldn't predict that your friend would have try to kill himself with a pencil sharpener."

Logi's tone was sarcastic and I didn't like it at all. The situation seemed to me decidedly ambiguous. Siggi instead watched us amused until he received a call, at the end of which he reiterated what Logi had just told me.

"Don't worry, they took him to the infirmary. The doctor has already said that it's nothing serious. It's just a superficial cut. When he gets better, we'll let you know, but now it's better if you go back home."

I wanted to protest, mainly because no one had noticed the penknife, but I decided to keep calm.

"We will get back to you as soon as possible. One of our patrol cars will take you back to Reykjavík."

I went back down the long corridor and hurried away towards the exit. Unable to rebel against their arbitrary will, all I could do was obey and go back to Vesturbær.

5 GHOSTS OF THE PAST

Leaving Litla-Hraun prison, I boarded a white Volvo with red-blue side stripes. It was a car belonging to the Icelandic police car park. The driving agent was called Ási Jónsson.

He was a guy in his fifties, quite sociable and with peculiar features. His face reminded me of an elf: in fact, he had pointed ears and eyes of intense green colour. As usual, I began to fantasize and formulate bizarre theories about it. For example, I imagined that the Hidden People and the Icelanders had once united in marriage, and hybrid creatures like him, with human-elven features, were born from their relationship. Fortunately, Ási didn't take long to break the ice between us, and consequently he interrupted these imaginative thoughts. In just five minutes I was sitting next to him, he had told me he was married to Margrét, a nurse working for Landspitali (the national university hospital), and with whom he had two beautiful daughters, named Junia and Flora. He drank with moderation over the weekend, and he preferred Irish beers, especially pasteurized and filtered ones. His favourite football team was Liverpool, but he sympathized with Leiknir, a local second division club.

"In Iceland, football is called *fótbolti*, and it is a sport followed by everyone. Our national teams, both male and female, have achieved excellent positions in recent years and I am sure that one day we will win an international trophy," he said with some pride.

He then asked me about my favourite club, and I naturally replied that it was S.S.C. Napoli.

"I remember when Diego Armando Maradona and Antonio Careca played for your team. At that time S.S.C. Napoli was really invincible," the policeman said enthusiastically.

Ási even told me about an episode related to the Hidden People that he had witnessed when he was a child. I was so excited to listen to his story. This type of episode had a unique value for me because it was personally experienced by those who were reporting it to me. As I listened carefully, I tried to memorize the details of his testimony which I considered interesting for my studies on Icelandic folklore. His direct experience would be part of an interesting stories database later.

It was not a legend, or a story handed down without any verification, but an encounter that I would define as a close encounter of the third kind, exactly like in the case of UFO sightings.

"I was 10 years old at the time. That weekend I stayed at Grandpa Gunnar's house. As usual, Grandpa came to greet me in my bedroom before I fell asleep. As soon as he left the room, I remember that I was there with my eyes still open, immersed in my thoughts. The room was illuminated by the yellowish light of a lamp resting on the bedside table next to me. In the corner, there was a large stone, a real boulder, which Gunnar thought not to remove from the guestroom."

"Why?" I instinctively asked.

"The elves would get angry. That was their home and should not be touched. So said my grandfather, who believed in these things."

In the Hafnarfjörður area, there are old wooden houses from the 1800s, where you can come across huge boulders inside a room, just as Ási was telling me. Curiously, the owners of these houses do not remove them to avoid the 'protests' of the Huldufólk. These rocks became like a piece of bedroom furniture.

"Following the thread of my thoughts, I observed, without paying too much attention, the leaves of a climbing plant placed to cover that rock. Surprisingly I saw that they started moving. I opened my eyes to see better, with the heart that had begun to beat more than normal. The leaves of the plant were really moving and continued with a slight rustle. So, I raised my head slightly from the pillow, I moved aside the covers a little to lean forward, and I saw him. He was an elf and did not look at all reassuring, indeed in all honesty his features were decidedly unpleasant. His mouth and eyes were huge compared to the rest of the body. He was no taller than 90 cm. He dressed in medieval clothes, like the ones you will have seen in storybooks."

This detail made me think of Snorri and our meeting in the fjord park.

"It happened to me, too. I met one of those creatures. But unlike you, this elf didn't frighten me at all; on the contrary, he seemed rather friendly," I commented interrupting his story.

"Very interesting. Perhaps it means you are welcome in Iceland," he said smugly.

"Then what happened? Did he talk to you?" I asked curiously.

"He looked at me insistently and seemed to whisper something incomprehensible. He did something, however, which allowed me to understand that he had no bad intentions: he smiled at me. While listening to the beating of my heart, I found myself unwittingly calling my grandfather Gunnar. I was still terrified. The elf disappeared even before the echo of my call had gone. I told my grandfather that I had seen "someone" at that particular point on the plant, but he didn't believe me, or he simply pretended not to believe me to avoid frightening me any further.

Making sure that I had calmed down, he returned to his bedroom, but the elf never appeared again. That was the only time."

"Wow, what a story!"

Ási's anecdote certainly enriched my knowledge of these mysterious apparitions. Meanwhile, outside it was raining and blowing strong wind, but we were both so taken, that we didn't pay attention to the bad weather conditions. Consequently, the return home was really relaxing, as it allowed me to distract myself from the deep pain I felt at that time for the murder of Lena and for the possible guilt of my friend Marco.

"Where exactly do you live?"

"In Vesturbær, not far from Vesturbæjarlaug, the public swimming pool," I replied as if it was the most obvious thing in the world.

"I live in Breiðholt, but I know your neighbourhood well. My daughter works on weekends in a pastry shop in Hofsvallagata. You probably know that they make an extremely delicious *snúður*!"

"I've never been there, but I know which pastry shop you are referring to. Maybe next time I'll try it for sure." When we entered my district, the anxiety generated by the events that occurred in the last twenty-four hours returned. My first thought was for Lena, the second one went to Marco. Both were victims of a fate greater than themselves. Upon greeting Ási, the agent got out of the car and hugged me warmly.

"This is the *rosahringur minni* that will protect you from the evil around us."

He offered me a *galdrastafir*, painted on a piece of wood, and depicting a protective circle. I was speechless. I gladly accepted the gift and thanked him for giving me a ride out to my house. Ási was a special person; maybe he had simply sensed my mood and wanted to cheer me up with that friendly gesture. When I took the keys from a jacket pocket, the policeman got back into the car and drove off slowly. I was happy to see once again that empathy, the ability to understand and share the feelings of another, has no nationality.

After all, human beings should never be stereotyped on the basis of their geographical and cultural background; better have an opinion based on personal experiences. I entered the door and went up the stairs of the condominium where I lived. When I opened the door of my apartment, I went directly to the bathroom to wash my hands. Then I rinsed my face with warm water, which in Iceland is characterized by a very slight smell of rotten eggs due to its geothermal origin. After the cleaning ritual was over, I went to the kitchen to prepare something to eat. I didn't want to waste time, I was so hungry, and I opted for a quick dish: spaghetti with tomato sauce, which I would have flavoured with precious grated parmesan cheese. 'Precious' because Parmigiano-Reggiano is an expensive product; its price, in fact, is extremely high here in Iceland compared to the Italian standard. The trip to the 'North Pole' (as my mother would say) is long enough, that I willingly and agreeably accept such additional costs, especially when I am homesick.

However, any Italian product are available in the Icelandic supermarkets, such as mozzarella, fresh pasta, aged cheeses, as well as our traditional cakes (like tiramisu, for example), and in some periods of the year even *gnocchi*, sent directly from a pasta factory in Campania, my native region. When I was finally about to put the first forkful of spaghetti in my mouth, I received a call.

"Valentino..."

"I don't hear you well."

None of my acquaintances had Birna's number, except her and Ingi the lawyer.

"Do you remember what I told you in Naples?"

The line was constantly interrupted, and the panting breath of that woman made our communication even more complicated. It was clear that Marco's aunt was not on the other side of the phone. It was a familiar voice, but I couldn't recognize it. I couldn't put a name to the voice.

"Sorry, I don't understand what you mean. Can you repeat it, please?"

"They will try to perform the ritual, but this time they will make one last diabolical miracle to close the circle and to control the mind of the sacrificed one."

Only then did I understand who I was talking to. According to the Swiss psychoanalyst Carl Jung, ghosts have always been close to human beings and exert an invisible but powerful influence on them. Although not everyone can perceive the presence of these ethereal entities, I personally have witnessed inexplicable events and have heard stories about it since childhood. It would seem that the souls of the deceased who have not received an appropriate burial, or those who have been victims of violent death, are condemned as a consequence of wandering the world of the living as ghosts. Other times restless souls would manifest themselves because they were driven by a bond of love, which would not be interrupted with their death. I finally realized that she was Gudrun. I was sure, absolutely sure at this point.

"You must help me find the light. *Draumfarir tíðar, mun hurðum upp ljúka!*"

Something about her struck me as spiritual, even before I remembered the meaning of the sentence in Icelandic: 'Lucid dreams will eventually open the portal'.

"Gudrun, how can I help you?"

No reply. The phone call had ended abruptly. It was all happening so fast that I didn't have time to reflect and deal with the ghosts of the past. Instead, I instinctively wrote a message to Father Ramón. The only one who could probably understand me. I needed to confide in someone who was familiar with 'lost souls'. The priest was certainly the right person who could address these matters.

Dear Father Ramón,

it was a pleasure to meet you this morning.

Unfortunately, the aftermath of the day was horrendous.

The police arrested a friend of mine for the murder of his girlfriend. I need to talk to you; will you meet me somewhere?

After about twenty minutes I received his reply, and for a moment I felt heartened.

Dear Valentino,

Thanks for your message, I had already learned from the television the terrible news of the murder of that poor girl. I am praying for you and also for your friends. Evil is among us, alas. As I said, the earth is infested with unclean creatures that often tempt and seduce us with their diabolical miracles. These evil spirits are dangerous and hate humans. I could dwell on this topic, but we will discuss it better closely. You are welcome here at the Cathedral. We can meet tomorrow afternoon. I am free around 3 o'clock. Remember that you can always count on me.

God bless you.

In faith,

Father Ramón Vasquez Vicario

A moment later the anxiety returned fiercely. Unexpectedly, instead of reassuring me, the priest's letter raised and increased my apprehension, amplifying my fears. I was aware that I had stumbled upon a nightmare story, but this time it was real and not just a bad dream.

6 THE RETURN OF THE SORCERERS

The next day, when I woke up, I had a cup of instant espresso coffee. I drank it all in one gulp. Apparently, I hadn't heard the alarm ringing. Not having enough time to take a shower, I washed at the sink and I got ready as fast as I could. After that, I dressed, and I was soon out of the door. I was expected to give a lecture at the university.

Despite the terrible events that had shaken me, I had regained some of my self-control. As I walked, I thought about the topics I would discuss during the morning seminar. Today's lesson was scheduled for nine o'clock. The lecture would concern the spread of Christianity in Iceland, which occurred through a slow but progressive conversion of the pre-existing Pagan symbols with those of the Christian tradition. For example, the symbols of the Church, such as the cross and its variations, including the monogram of Christ, gradually replaced the images of wild animals and Pagan deities of the Viking iconography. Since this was a topic that I considered interesting, I also expected large participation from my students. The faculty of Social and Cultural Anthropology was not far from the crime scene. Passing through Suðurgata, I thought I saw someone inside Marco's villa. I went to the gate to take a closer look. I stayed there for a couple of minutes, hoping to see something.

By focusing on a few details, I realized that I was wrong. The crime scene tapes had not been removed from the front door nor from the other fixtures. I clearly saw that all the seals were still intact so that nobody could enter without removing them. Perhaps it was only my imagination.

"False alarm," I thought.

I looked around and noticed that a girl with oriental features was looking at me circumspectly across the street. She must have been seven years old. Her hair was pitch black, and her forehead was covered up with bangs. She reminded me of a favourite character of mine in the Japanese anime world: Lana, a young lady from a post-apocalyptic science fiction anime series titled *Future Boy Conan*. When she was a few meters away from me, she spoke to me.

"Have you seen the shadows too?"

I was freaking out, but I smiled at her. The girl was a weirdo and behaved in a bizarre, creepy, spooky way. I don't want to overdo it, but it was like watching a scene from a scary movie by director Hideo Nakata.

I began to suspect something supernatural with regard to the mysterious girl. I had the confirmation when she said with a loud voice something that scared me even more.

"The ghost of a woman just told me you have to hurry. You're the one who has to help her find the light."

I gasped loudly and let out an almost guttural moan of fear. My heart rate sped up while my body froze. I wasn't sure how to behave and what to say to her. In the end, I opted for another fake smile, but I hid my disquieting feelings of anguish and uneasiness. 'Lana' continued to stare at me impassively. I suddenly realized that I was late for my lesson, so I turned my back to her, and I continued at a fast pace. Surely this meeting was not a coincidence. I convinced myself that I had come again across a phenomenon that transcended reality. Perhaps it could be connected with the phone call I received the previous evening. What if Gudrun was the entity who wanted to interact with me? I had some perceptions, but I was looking for certainties.

Reflecting on these thoughts, I arrived at the university campus. As I crossed the tree-lined avenue leading to the central building where my classroom was located, I met a group of anthropology students. One of them recognized me. He stopped me and said:

"Valentino, the department got flooded. Probably classes are suspended for today."

The guy was right. A fire-engine tanker stopped in front of the main entrance of the University of Iceland, while a dozen brigades were working to locate a leak in the exhaust pipes. The damage had to be significant. Shortly after, the rector confirmed to me the situation. Upon entering the rector's office, Jón Magnússon greeted me with one of his warm hugs. He was nominated as rector of the faculty of anthropology a few weeks before. Jón had been my doctoral thesis supervisor. As an expert on runes, the old alphabet used by the ancient Germanic peoples, the professor was known throughout the academic world for his studies. He and his wife Fanney helped me a lot during my first experience in Iceland.

After a while, Jón gave me the bad news that even more adversely affected my balance and tension levels.

"Valentino minn, I'm sorry to tell you right now, but someone stole from the library the 16th-century manuscript you were studying. Someone took it away taking advantage of the confusion. The casket where it was kept has been broken into."

He was referring to an ancient grimoire he translated from Latin but which he had not been able to fully decipher. A textbook of magic dating back to the Middle Ages, typically including instructions on how to create magical objects like talismans and amulets, how to perform magical spells, charms and divination, and how to summon or invoke supernatural entities such as angels, spirits, deities and demons. The University of Iceland had the original version from a Brighton museum to allow me to closely analyse some mysterious symbols.

"Don't worry about the manuscript, I have already reported the fact to the police. Tomorrow I will inform the museum director myself."

"Well, I'm shocked," I said frankly.

"We have another problem to solve in the next few hours. I was constricted to suspend all the teaching activities for at least a week. The firefighters cannot locate the leak position. They told me they will need to work the whole day. And moreover, in the end, we will have to clean and disinfect the entire building. I guess it will take days, if not weeks, to make the university accessible to students again."

I felt like crying, then I felt like yelling. After a long, tedious effort for months, I finally had gotten the authorization to borrow the manuscript, but now everything's messed up. Mine was a wave of generalized anger. I started crying and I couldn't stop. The situation was getting out of hand. I could no longer control myself, but Jón was extremely kind to me.

"Forgive me if I did not contact you yesterday. I'm close to you and I'm here to help, Valentino. To do whatever I can to make things easier," said the Professor.

"Listen, Jón, I'm sorry for the outburst, but I have never experienced so many troubles during such a short time period since I moved to Iceland," I admitted, disheartened.

He placed his left hand over my shoulder telling me to calm down and reassuring me that everything would be fine.

"If today was a bad day, wait a few days: it will probably be better tomorrow. Once everything is settled, we will meet again."

He dismissed me with that sibylline sentence. I wiped away the tears, said goodbye and left the room. It was too early for the appointment with Father Ramón and, in any case, I wanted to spend the rest of the morning alone. So I decided to go downtown to my favourite café, the *Stúdiókaffi*. It was urgent to rearrange ideas over a cup of steaming cappuccino, but my phone rang and then my plans changed again. Those days were so intense that I felt like a puppet in the hands of a puppeteer who quickly moved me from one side of the stage to the other. I felt as though I had no control over the events unfolding.

"*Saell* Valentino. I'm Ingi, Birna's lawyer."

"Good morning."

"Sorry if I disturb you. Can we meet?"

"Yes, we can. I am available right now."

"Very well. Are you familiar with Vesturbær district?"

"Of course, it's the neighbourhood where I live."

"Then come to my house. It's in Hagamelur 3. I'll wait for you."

"Okay. See you in about twenty minutes."

So I went straight to Ingi's house. It was not difficult to find his apartment. I went to the door and knocked.

"Come in!" Said a voice from inside.

I went in and Ingi greeted me with a handshake.

"Please, sit on that armchair. Do you want coffee?"

"Yes please."

He went into the kitchen and returned to the living room with a thermos that seemed uninviting to me. In fact, it wasn't the coffee I would have expected, but I politely accepted a cup. After all, I had become accustomed to drinking Scandinavian *Ciofeca*'s without batting an eyelid. With the word *Ciofeca*, the Italians designate a disgusting thing of poor quality. In Naples, espresso coffee is incredibly tasty, but in Iceland, I had to accept, let's say, the diversity of flavour.

"Is there any news?" I asked with apprehension.

"I visited Marco in his cell this morning. The wound he has sustained will heal in a few days. He seemed calm, but certainly affected by being in the prison."

"Was that all you wanted to say to me?"

"No. Actually there is more. When I was about to leave, Marco jumped up from his chair and approached me saying:

"You must know, dear lawyer, that there is someone who wanted to insult my origin and my culture. I was caught in the act, but for a crime that I did not commit at all! I'm innocent, you have to believe me!"

"Valentino, there was something disturbing in his eyes that deeply frightened me. He looked around to see if anyone could listen to us; then he took my arm and said:

"The Sorcerers of Hólmavík assassinated my lovely Lena!"

"Believe me, I really thought he was crazy," the Icelandic attorney commented astonished.

I almost jumped out of my chair. The Sorcerers of Hólmavík was an old acquaintance of mine; an elite of persons who have acquired great financial, political and religious influence over the centuries. And to make matters worse, the sect would use black magic to contact the Hidden People to obtain earthly benefits. All of this increased the aura of mystery that surrounded Lena Piotrowska's death. Consequently, I convinced myself that Marco could be truly innocent; so he did not tell the lawyer any imaginative lies over and above truth and facts. Ingi obviously thought differently.

"Yesterday Marco was totally out of his mind. I believed that he was under the influence of alcohol or drugs. Perhaps he was just in a state of deep depression. In this eventuality, the judge could reduce the penalty if I could demonstrate his incapability at the time of committing the murder."

"Are you joking?" I replied contemptuously to his conclusions.

"I'm very sorry, I understand your disappointment, but I think the only viable defensive strategy that comes to my mind is to ask for the infirmity of my client, although on the surface it may not appear to be so," said the lawyer coldly.

In the end, I pretended to agree with him so as not to give the impression that I really believed in the existence of the sect. I knew that I was moving in an irrational context, but I was the only one who could exonerate Marco. However, I could not abandon him to his fate; so I decided that I would investigate the matter on my own. I said goodbye to Ingi and I left his apartment.

"Goodbye, lawyer. I will inform Birna about our meeting."

"Okay. Goodbye Valentino. I will try to do everything possible that is good for Marco."

7 DEVILS, BONES AND DEMONIC POSSESSIONS

Although it seemed clear to me that the murder of Lena Piotrowska, apart from the official truth that was inexorably emerging, would not have been an easy solution, I was still motivated to extricate myself from the few elements I had available. As I reflected on what I learned from the lawyer, I realized that I still had four hours of waiting.

It was about eleven o'clock and the appointment with the priest was scheduled for three in the afternoon. I just had to retake the old plan, so I decided to go for a coffee at the Stúdiókaffi. The cafeteria was deserted because at that time of day most Icelanders were at work or school. The tourists, instead, were probably busy taking photos during some organized excursion among mighty geysers and suggestive autumn landscapes. I didn't lose heart and went to talk to the nice bartender, a girl from the Czech Republic.

"Good morning Valentino, what can I serve you?"

Jana was a sociable girl and it was fun to exchange jokes with her that always put me in a good mood. This morning she was not very talkative and she just took the order. After asking her to prepare me the usual cappuccino with a double espresso, I sat down at a table located near the same windowsill where I had previously met Father Ramón. I remembered putting a notebook into my bag before leaving my apartment to walk to the university.

I had the idea of making a sort of list of the events more or less inherent to the murder of Lena together with the names of all the people I had met in the last few days. I started with the individual episodes which I then analysed in detail one by one:

I. *Marco's anomalous behaviour the evening before the murder;*

II. *The first meeting with Judge Siggi;*

III. *The "premonitory" nightmare;*

IV. *The meeting with Father Ramón at the cafeteria;*

V. *Marco's house and the crowd of onlookers;*

VI. *The assassination of Lena;*

VII. *The visit to Litla-Hraun prison and Marco's attempted suicide;*

VIII. *The chat with the policeman Ási;*

IX. *The theft of the manuscript;*

X. *The Sorcerers of Hólmavík and their possible involvement in the murder.*

I. *Sigurður Bjarni Baldursson (Siggi):*
Freemason and judge of the Reykjavík district court; he is responsible for the preliminary investigations. He speaks good Italian and has a villa in Tuscany.

II. *Padre Ramón Vasquez Vicario:*
Jesuit priest and expert on diabolical miracles.

III. *Logi Ragnarsson:*
police chief and arrogant person; he is convinced of Marco's guilt.

IV. *Ási Jónsson:*
policeman and sweet man who believes in the existence of the Hidden People.

V. *Ingi Berg Guðmundsson:*
lawyer and friend of Birna; he is probably a Freemason and perhaps a sympathizer of Nazism. He too was convinced of Marco's guilt.

In hindsight, I realized that Marco's behaviour could have been manipulated by someone or something. His attitude was definitely an element that left me perplexed. Not that it could presage his murderous intentions, but it was certainly unusual as I knew him. It was not like him to act in that rude and aggressive manner. After analysing the situation, I was more than sure that the nightmare I had the night before it could be actually a premonition to alert me of Lena's death. On the other hand, both my encounters with Father Ramón and Ási did not seem to me in any way episodes to be considered useful for a resolution of the case. By the way, I found weird the attitude of Siggi and Logi following Marco's suicide attempt. During the first meeting with judge Siggi, I had occasion to find that he was a nice guy, but suddenly I had a doubt. What if he followed us on purpose to that club? Maybe he wanted to make sure Marco was ready to make that insane gesture; however, I couldn't find any justifiable reason for it.

The possible involvement of the sect worried me a lot. I had omitted Birna from the list and I ended up eliminating from the suspicious profiles both Father Ramón and Ási the policeman. Of course, from a conspiracy point of view, anyone could be a member of the Sorcerers of Hólmavík, even the loving Aunt Birna. However, I hoped that if there was a "sorcerer" among the people I mentioned, he would most likely have been an individual who held leading roles, and not men of faith or simple penitentiary agents such as Ramón and Ási. The judge and lawyer, for example, were both Freemasons and were part of Reykjavík's high society. They certainly could have been potential "sorcerers". The police chief, the arrogant Logi, although he was an influential person, did not appear to me to belong (or at least not in a clear way) to any Masonic Lodge. Nevertheless, his lack of doubts about Marco's guilt made me think of his attempt to cover up something. He too could be a member of the sect.

Why was I rambling like this? I had simply time to waste until that meeting and I decided to spend it speculating upon suspicious profiles. I must admit, however, that I did not have the right tools to carry out a real investigation. I wasn't a professional detective but I expected Father Ramón to offer me advice and suggestions on my numerous queries. I didn't know him well enough, but he had given me the impression of being a wise man to trust, and a dispenser of good advice. I would have talked to him about the "sorcerers" and my theories, perhaps exaggerated, but not so far-fetched, on their possible hidden motives; and in addition, I would have told him about Gudrun and the inexplicable phenomena that had occurred in the past few hours. I put the notebook back in the bag and I prepared for the appointment with him at the cathedral. Landakotskirkja was the main Catholic place of worship in the city, where masses were celebrated in Icelandic, English, Latin, and Polish. Speaking of languages, I remembered that Lena was volunteering at weekends, giving free Icelandic lessons to children of immigrants.

"Maybe Father Ramón saw her sometime during her volunteer service," I said thinking aloud, "and who knows he may have noticed something unusual around the church lately."

I set off again and in five minutes I arrived outside the cathedral. The entrance was at the base of a tower with a bell tower. The door was open and I entered. The interior had an immense Latin cross plan, as the two arms of the transept were shorter than the nave. Continuing towards the high altar, I noticed that there was no trace of the priest. So I looked for him in the sacristy, hoping to find him there. He wasn't even in his office. But having ascertained that Father Ramón had not arrived, I decided to wait for him sitting on one of the wooden benches. Another half-hour passed, during which a wealthy middle-aged American tourist couple had entered the Church. Tired of waiting, I decided to write a message and leave it on a table near the altar.

Dear Father Ramón, I came here for our appointment.
See you another time.
Greetings Valentino.

All of a sudden, a breath of freezing air hit me. There was a mechanical noise, like a gear that had started. One of the walls of the tabernacle was slowly opening behind me, and in a matter of seconds, it revealed a secret passage. The passage led through the wooden steps to an underground from which a strong smell of sulphur came. After a few moments, something happened that upset me. I heard a male voice inviting me to go downstairs.

"Valentino, come and help me!"

I had no intention of descending those infernal steps and yet I found myself thrown from below by an invisible force. I was unable to control my body.

My legs and hands trembled so badly; they were in excruciating pain and difficult to control. My brain was out of control: I was suffocating, struggling to breathe. All I knew was that I was in a very scary place. I was terrified of the whole situation. I could hear some noise in the distance that I couldn't quite distinguish. I realized the presence of a large number of human bones scattered everywhere. I was probably in a crypt; it was a damp place but strangely lit by numerous candles. I took courage and got up. As I was about to move up again, I saw three moving silhouettes coming out of the darkness from one of the corridors in the basement. At first glance, they seemed to me three men intent on dragging something. Fear took over and I felt paralyzed. As they approached me, the stench of sulphur increased in intensity. They were no longer blurred shadows, but demonic figures. I had only one chance to alleviate terror, namely closing my eyes, the only organs over which I still had control. It didn't help much. They started tearing up, perhaps because of the unpleasant smell that came from those diabolical creatures.

One of them was Haagenti. He was a fallen angel who commanded thirty-three legions of demons. He is generally depicted as a big bull with the wings of a griffin, but that day he appeared in human form. His voice was indescribable, deep and inhuman.

"Have you ever wondered about the meaning of your nightmares?"

Haagenti was able to control people's dreams, causing serious anxiety during the daytime and insomnia during the night-time. Next to him was his brother Berith, a demon who had the power to push men to commit murders.

"Are you sure Marco killed Lena?" He asked me with a disturbing grin.

Berith appeared as a soldier dressed in red, riding a horse of the same colour and wore a king's crown on his head. The third demon instead was able to reveal secrets and facts about the past, present, and future of human beings. His name was Vassago, a demon described in demonological grimoires such as the Lesser Key of Solomon and the Book of the Office of Spirits.

"Help her, lead her to the light. You'll see, she will reward you. But watch out for the priest-kings," he said, looking me straight in the eye.

Suddenly the three devils turned away and picked up from the ground what they had dragged up there. It was a dead body. They started hitting him violently, dismembered him and swallowed his bones, one by one. I was the eyewitness to a creepy show. It was all done on the spur of the moment. Then I saw three men arriving from one of the underground tunnels, shouting like crazy.

"What do you want? Did you come to ruin us?" The three men said simultaneously.

Looking at them closely, I understood that they were possessed by the three devils. In fact, they seemed to be out of their mind and moved like spiders from one wall to the other of the crypt. They wriggled on the ground and took on expressions of anger and pain. I watched them in amazement and horrified. I was helpless and unable to free myself from my fears and from a situation that had nothing rational.

I prayed for a miracle, for a divine intervention that would rescue me. I had already seen what I was experiencing now in the nightmare of the past few days. It had been, as I suspected, a premonitory dream. In Christianity, demons are fallen angels, who sided with Satan and were cast out of heaven. This is written in the Bible, in the book of Revelation (12: 9):

"And the great dragon was cast out, that old serpent, called the Devil, and Satan, which deceived the whole world: he was cast out into the earth, and his angels were cast out with him."

On the other hand, I was thrown by a dark force into the basement of the cathedral, inside a crypt illuminated by the light of hundreds of candles. I started praying with great faith, but there was no way to get them away from me. I closed my eyes and at that point, I lost consciousness.

8 THE MARCH OF THE PRIEST-KINGS

Who were all those people in the Indian row in front of me? I followed them because I had no other choice. I was the last of the line and behind me, there was the void. For sure, I was no longer under the cathedral's crypt, not anymore.

This place was like a timeless dimension suspended in the cosmos, light years away from the planet earth. "Don't think too much but live the experience fully!" Said a man dressed in black in front of me. "What do you mean?" I asked, confused. No answer. I was walking along with that myriad of men dressed in black towards an unknown destination. The sky above us was dark and the thunder was constant and threatening. Maybe I had fallen asleep and I was dreaming. A dream which I feared could turn into a nightmare at any moment. Continuing along that one-way path, after a time lapse that seemed to be an eternity, we arrived at the end of that floating road. There was a huge square surrounded by very high walls. The men in black formed a ritual circle. I had the feeling that they knew what to do and how to behave. At the centre of the square, there was a huge black swastika.

Looking at it better, I realized that was not a swastika, but it appeared more like a large crumpled diamond. A tall man ordered to put eighteen wooden structures in some specific points of the square. They were eighteen gigantic runes made by wooden strains. "Let's begin the ritual," commanded the same man with a solemn voice. The followers used fiery torches to burn them. It was an impressive and suggestive show. The sequel was even surprising for its development. A woman was dragged in the middle of the scene. She was wearing a *Faldobúningur*, a traditional dress worn by Icelandic women between the seventeenth and the nineteenth century. The name of the dress derived from its headgear, which had a long-curved plume, called *Spaðafaldur*. In its most recognized form, it incorporated a hat decorated with a curved sheet-like ornament protruding into the air.

I was struck by the beauty of that girl. Her face looked familiar, but I didn't have a clue who she was. Her eyes were magnetic, of a grey-green colour. She wore a silver necklace and silver earrings as well. I stared at her and then realized that I knew her very well. And, yes, of course, I recognized her. She was my Gudrun!

"Give the boy the athamé."

The guy who gave the orders nodded, and a young man was led in front of Gudrun. She was lying on an improvised altar, consisting of a pentagonal stone slab. Her body was sprinkled with rose petals. At that point they passed a dagger to the boy, the athamé precisely, a particular knife used in pagan rituals. It is a ceremonial blade, generally with a black handle. It is the main ritual implement or magical tool among several used in ceremonial magic traditions, and by other neopagans, witchcraft, as well as satanic traditions. Still, the dynamics of events suggested that human sacrifice was about to be fulfilled. I was baffled when I saw the face of the boy.

We were two of a kind. He had my same face. It at first felt odd, like running into a twin brother. As I watched him stunned, the ritual just began. The tall man who gave the orders shouted a magic formula in Latin:

"Diem ex die facultatem sentiendi augeo et veneficium penìtus didìco."

My double acted as if he were in a trance, so he had no control over his actions. Then he began to stab Gudrun's body. The boy was like a puppet, dominated by a dark force that rendered his will null. The young woman was stabbed to death.

"Our earthly benefits will be renewed for another one hundred and eighty years. So it has been, and it will be forever," said the tall man.

At that precise moment, I saw a new scenario before my eyes. I was in a cemetery and my attention came to a funeral inscription.

IN MEMORY OF VALENTINO VOTO
1979-2019

Time passes, love remains
Until the daybreak, and the shadows flee away

"Valentino. Valentino."

I heard a voice calling me repeatedly, it seemed warm and affable to me.

"Who are you? What do you want from me?" I asked, still dazed by those shocking visions.

The man took something from a table that was nearby. I could not understand what it was immediately. I waited a few seconds, observing the scene that seemed to be slowed down.

"Drink some, but not everything," he said, handing me a glass.

It was a glass of lukewarm but thirst-quenching water that I sipped as if it were a magic potion with an invigorating effect. I was slowly regaining control of my senses and my mind. It was only after a few minutes that I understood who was that kind man.

"Father Ramón, I am so glad you see you."

"I was really worried because you looked like you were in agony, and I couldn't wake you up."

"I had terrible nightmares and I think I had difficulty discerning them from reality," I justified my mental state to the priest.

"Do you remember what exactly happened?"

"I was waiting for your arrival and then I remember falling into the crypt."

"The crypt? What do you mean? This cathedral has no crypt," replied Father Ramón in amazement.

When I realized the absurdity of what I had just experienced, the situation became embarrassing. I was afraid I wasn't believed by the priest. I even thought I hit my head somewhere, causing irreparable brain damage. I was extremely confused.

"Were there any demons in your nightmares?"

"Exactly. How do you know?" I asked, surprised.

Ramón looked at me with satisfaction but he did not answer my question. How did he know what I had just dreamed of? He smiled, but he still didn't want to give me explanations. Then, finally, given my concern, he gave me an answer.

"The devils are everywhere, especially in nightmares. That's why I immediately thought of them."

The affair was as from the beginning rather tangled and enigmatic. The constant twists and turns were certainly upsetting for my psyche, but at the same time stimulating. I wanted to investigate both mysteries with the Jesuit: the murder of Lena and the apparitions of Gudrun. Were there any connections between the two episodes? Or was it my subconscious that wanted to warn me of something? Were these premonitions sort of pieces of evidence for the paranormal nature of dreams?

9 DIABOLICAL SECRETS

I wished I could find in Father Ramón advice, affection and understanding. Then I told him everything I remembered and witnessed during my last dream activity. I told him it was a devastating experience for me. It felt comfortable to confide in him.

---

[4] Ninurta with his thunderbolts pursues Anzû stealing the Tablet of Destinies from Enlil's sanctuary (Austen Henry Layard Monuments of Nineveh, 2nd Series, 1853).

"Three demons, Haagenti, Berith and Vassago appeared to me in that dream. I was terrified by their gaze, even though I had the feeling that they wanted to warn me of something. Maybe they wanted to help me."

"Come on, Valentino. Don't be silly. The devils don't help anyone, at best they manipulate reality as they please," he said interrupting me.

Nonetheless, that was my perception. I, therefore, confessed to him my suspicion that behind the death of Lena could be the Sect of the Sorcerers of Hólmavík. Ramón ruled out this hypothesis. He was much more inclined to believe that Marco had been seduced and manipulated by the devil, unaware victim of a transcendental power that could not be defeated with the help of lawyers and judges. He denied the existence of such a secret society that could control and cloud the human mind through the use of black magic. I was struck by his words and invited him to continue, but I still tried to understand if the ritual I saw in that dream was somehow connected with the murder of Lena.

It was important to understand if Marco had any chance to prove his innocence, despite being the material perpetrator of that crime. I insisted on my conspiracy thesis and asked him a question about the priest-kings.

"The demon named Vassago told me to watch out for the king-priests. Have you ever heard of it?"

"Of course, it is often mentioned in the Old Testament. For example, Melchidesech was a famous king-priest, an emblematic and mysterious figure. He was the king of the kingdom of Salem and at the same time Priest of the very high Elyon, one of the Hebrew names of God. But I believe that neither the sect nor the priest-kings have anything to do with the death of that poor girl," he commented with a cordial smile.

At the end of my story, the Jesuit explained exactly what is meant by a diabolical miracle and what powers have demons. I was tired and upset, but it was worth listening to.

"I once saw a devil holding a ritual dagger, the athamé, next to a statue of the Virgin Mary. I was not dreaming and it was not an imaginary vision. That demon was called Aamon and he told me that he was much stronger than a human being because he had largely kept the gifts of his angelic nature. Oh, but beware, demons are still creatures of the Lord. They are not omnipotent like him, but simply retain the extraordinary power of angels. Aamon was in the mood for confidences that day, and he revealed to me that Satan and his followers cannot produce any supernatural phenomenon since they have no faculty. Being creatures of the Lord, they are not able to create something out of nothing as He would. In addition, they do not have the ability to raise the dead or heal the sick people as Jesus did once."

"So what are they able to do?"

"They could pretend to resurrect a dead, creating an illusion, a sort of mirage. They could go through material substances and even pretend to be able to predict what will happen in the future. These are rather accurate but not certain predictions about a future event.

God knows all things, past, present, and future. Demons instead can only mislead us by creating conjectures. Diabolical miracles are nothing more than lies that a man of faith can always unmask; they are specifically amazing events that mean nothing. They aim to mystify and confuse pious souls like yours. They manifest themselves in words, thoughts and acts contrary to the law of God and the teachings of Jesus. Evidently the faith of your friend Marco was not so strong, that's why he fell into temptation."

I also started to talk to him about Gudrun and her inexplicable apparitions, but he immediately stopped me.

"The Holy Bible teaches us that the human being can perform meritorious acts as long as he is alive. When death comes, he can no longer do anything for his own salvation. Ghosts do not exist. No dead person can return and interact with the living. I believe that you, Valentino, want to believe it. Maybe you feel lonely and you simply want a partner. You will see that when you have found serenity, a woman's love will also come."

Father Ramón demonstrated to me that he knew much more than I thought. Indeed he provided me with information that guided my investigation into a new direction. Aware that it could be a waste of time, I decided to deepen anyway the figure of Melchidesech and the other king-priests. Father Ramón, embracing me affectionately, dismissed me with this admonition:

"Be careful, Valentino. Don't mess with the devil and his infernal legions!"

After receiving his message, I said goodbye and went to the local library to look for documentary material on these topics. I walked to Landsbókasafn, the place where is kept the largest collection of books and manuscripts in Iceland. The main building of the complex is called Þjóðarbókhlaðan, a tall, bright, imposing, red and white building, located near the university campus. I was lucky, the closing time was at 22:00 so that I had enough time to carry out my research calmly. Reading rooms were usually frequented by students of all faculties.

The area where old books were kept was never crowded. When I entered the section of sacred texts, I saw only a couple of twenty-year-olds who had secluded in a corner. I immediately went to work. As Father Ramón anticipated, I found news about Melchidesech in the Old Testament. This is what is reported in the book of Genesis 14:18:

When Abram returned from his defeat of Chedorlaomer and the kings who were allied with him, the king of Sodom went out to greet him in the Valley of Shaveh. Melchizedek, king of Salem, brought out bread and wine. He was a priest of God Most High. He blessed Abram with these words: "Blessed be Abram by God Most High, the creator of heaven and earth, and blessed be God Most High, who delivered your foes into your hand". Then Abram gave him a tenth of everything.

Melchidesech is also mentioned in Psalm 110:

The Lord said unto my Lord: «Sit thou at my right hand, until I make thine enemies thy footstool». The Lord shall send the rod of thy strength out of Zion: «Rule thou in the midst of thine enemies. Thy people shall be willing in the day of thy power, in the beauties of holiness from the womb of the morning; thou hast the dew of thy youth». The Lord hath sworn, and will not repent, Thou art a priest for ever after the order of Melchizedek». The Lord at thy right hand shall strike through kings in the day of his wrath. e shall judge among the heathen; he shall fill the places with the dead bodies; he shall wound the heads over many countries. He shall drink of the brook in the way: therefore shall he lift up the head.

"These texts are not helpful at all!" I snorted irritably at the end of the reading.

There wasn't the kind of clue I hoped to find. But the truth is that I was looking for something but I didn't know what exactly.

Meanwhile, the closing time was approaching, warning me that it was time to go home. It started to rain while I was at the library.

"Sir," said a boyish voice, making me jump with fright.

I turned around, and to my surprise, I found myself in front of "Lana", the little girl I had met outside Marco's villa. But seeing her there, with her impenetrable black eyes and bangs on her forehead, made a tremendous effect.

"What are you doing here darling?" I asked frightened.

"Follow me," she said, looking at me fixedly, one palm from my face.

I can't understand how she managed to convince me, but I was forced to go after her like an automaton. I took my things and left the reading room at a brisk pace. The girl turned from time to time to check if I was following her.

"Where are we going so fast?" I questioned her while we were walking down a wet little street.

I asked again where she was taking me, but she didn't answer me. She merely brought a finger to her lips to silence me.

Although the situation was absurd and far-fetched, I was at the same time curious to see where it would lead me. So we went on for a while. Even though there was little light on the street and oddly the public lighting had not been turned on, I was able to glimpse the cemetery of Hólavallagarður from afar, whose name means "garden on a hill" in Icelandic. We kept walking for a few minutes until we reached inside the burial ground. Only then the little girl spoke to me again.

"I don't want to leave this place, but she wants it. She wants peace. You have to help her find the light."

She motioned me to look down and, to my dismay, I saw a tomb without ornaments and with an old wooden cross. On it was engraved in barely legible letters a name known to me, the years of birth and death, and a funerary inscription in Icelandic.

GUÐRÚN

1814 -1838

Á garði þessum grafin fyrst allra, 25. nóvember 1838

Maybe Gudrun had been buried in this cemetery and was using the girl to get in touch with me. It happened a lot, but I still didn't understand. What, exactly, did she want from me? Before disappearing into thin air, "Lana" gave me a clue.

"At three o'clock go to the deep part of the cathedral," she said as her body slowly dissolved like lava dust.

The girl was a ghost but I was already used to it; I was not surprised at all by that paranormal phenomenon. Suddenly, I remembered the crypt I had visited during the dream of the previous hours. Although Father Ramón had revealed to me that the cathedral did not have one, this circumstance, like all the other episodes so far, seemed to be somewhat bizarre.

I was even more intrigued and curious. The cathedral was not far from Hólavallagarður and I decided to go back there. When I arrived at the entrance, I didn't see anyone around and I didn't notice anything suspicious. It was midnight, but my incredible day was not over yet. I was about to head home when I heard a car approaching from a driveway in front of the sacristy. It was an Audi A7. I recognized in it the car that had previously followed me when I was with Siggi and Logi in the direction of the Litla-Hraun prison. I hid behind a low wall and glanced over the hedge. I saw three hooded people come out of the cockpit, one of whom opened a wooden door. They stopped to chat for a few seconds, then they sneaked into a room at the back of the cathedral. I followed them instinctively, being careful not to get noticed. Since the door hadn't been locked, I took the opportunity to go down a ramp. They seemed to me the steps of an endless staircase. However, I was not discouraged, I went all the way down exactly as Dante and Virgil did in the Divine Comedy to reach Hell.

I found myself at the end of the descent in a damp and ghostly place lit by candles. It was certainly a crypt. I was shocked: why had Father Ramón lied to me? The underground catacombs really existed. A group of masked people was intent on preparing a votive altar with the fire, incense, and entrails of an animal that I was unable to recognize; but the odd thing about it was that at first glance one would think that it was from a goat. There were about a dozen people in the *ambulatorium* when the Black Mass was about to begin. It was evident beyond any doubt that I had arrived in the middle of a satanic ritual, a parody of the Catholic Sunday mass. I was sure of it because the celebrants wore vestments similar to those of the priests but with the only difference that a demon was depicted on the tunic. In the Septuagint, the Greek translation of the Bible, the devil was described with horns, cloven hooves, unusually hairy legs, and a tail, often naked and holding a pitchfork. Consequently, the intentions of those gentlemen were clear to me. One of the masked men uttered the following Latin formula:

"*Adiutórium nostrum in nómine Dómini Inferi.*"

All the others responded with this greeting:

"*Ave Satanas!*"

I froze with fear; I was very scared and didn't know what to do, until, as was inevitable, I was noticed by one of the cult's followers.

"*Hver ertu?*" He asked me in Icelandic.

No response from me. Then the twist. Some of the disciples took off their masks, revealing their identity to me. I was shocked when I recognized their faces. The three hooded men I had followed down there in the catacombs were Professor Jón Magnússon, his wife Fanney and Birna, Marco's aunt. Far behind were Siggi and Logi, while Ingi the lawyer was next to a man who had not yet removed his mask. In an instant, all the old certainties were gone. I had unknowingly fallen into their trap.

Even though there were numerous clues, I wondered how I had managed not to notice anything. Where have I gone?

"I'll explain it to you," said someone behind me who inexplicably read my thoughts.

I turned abruptly and was incredulous that the person in front of me was Father Ramón. He looked at me with an indecipherable look. He took me by the hand and said:

"The time has finally come to speak to you. We have been following you everywhere for three years. You aged like a fine wine. I think this is the right time to reveal what you have the right to know for the success of the ritual. I tell you now that we are not the "sorcerers" you were looking for," he said with a sarcastic smile, arousing the hilarity of those present.

"So who are you?" I asked as if it mattered.

"We are the followers of the Light Bearer; we are the flatterers of the Supreme Master. He is our Morning Star; He is the holder of that wisdom that God has made inaccessible to the common man," he said in prey a disturbing euphoria.

I was furious and disappointed with myself for everything that was going on.

"Lucifer? But aren't you ashamed? You are a Jesuit, you belong to the elite order of the Catholic Church, you have made an oath of faith! Do you remember it?" I shouted at him in irrepressible anger.

"I remember that oath well:

"*To destroy heretics and their governments and rulers, and to spare neither age, nor sex, nor condition; to be as a corpse without any opinion or will of my own, but to implicitly obey my Superiors in all things without hesitation or murmuring...*"

But this is a dictatorship, it is pure material unhappiness. The Master instead only wants our well-being, our earthly happiness. What does God do instead from the heights of heaven? He is continuously vexing us with diseases and natural disasters. He cares little or nothing about our personal success and our "real" spiritual growth. Lucifer, on the contrary, is here with us on Earth; He is a nurturing father who does not neglect his children."

"What is this way of talking? Have you lost your mind? So you sold your soul to obtain earthly benefits, but you forgot one thing. The main objective of our earthly pilgrimage is to obtain the gift of eternal life through God's grace!" I said aloud, remembering the words of Father Santoro.

Jón intervened in the discussion:

"Valentino, don't be ridiculous with these rhetorical and meaningless phrases. We all went the other way because it was right to do it. Now stop behaving like an irresponsible child. The Master is a genuine soul. You will realize this as you become aware of your authentic self..."

The other followers nodded and looked at me as if I were a rebellious child to convince. I didn't want to give up my soul, but I was under attack. I calmed down and asked a dry question:

"So are you behind the murder of Lena Piotrowska?"

Jon and the priest looked at each other and said nothing more. Then Birna took over the conversation.

"Pay attention, please!"

The woman had a book in her hands which I recognized immediately. Apparently, they had stolen the 16th-century manuscript from the university library. And why had they done this? The answer was not long in coming. Birna opened a page of the book and pointed her finger at a magic formula written in Latin:

"*Diem ex die facultatem sentiendi augeo et veneficium penitus didico.*"

It was the ritual for mind control of the demon Aamon. They had used it to blur Marco's thoughts and to force him to commit that heinous murder. Immediately afterward his aunt explained better their evil intentions:

"Our cult has existed for millennia. To obtain gifts from our Master, there is a need for a human sacrifice to be made every 180 years. The ritual must involve a girl who must be killed by the one who loved her in life. Lena and Marco were perfect for the new ritual.

Sometimes twin souls reincarnate. You and Gudrun were perfect sometimes ago. This time you are reborn into the body of Valentino Voto. For us, this is a diabolical miracle because it shows continuity in our work. Your soul has returned to earth and Marco's soul will probably return in another 180 years to a new life. You are special and we need you to complete the ritual."

It was at that moment that Ingi and Logi brought a new-born baby to the middle of the votive altar. It was a gruesome scene. The baby-boy was crying desperately, while Jón drew esoteric symbols on his little body: the Armanen runes, a series of 18 runes that I had already seen in the dream of the king-priests.

"During the ceremony the child will be killed and you will slaughter him on the altar. His head will be placed on this table then, around the severed head, eighteen candles will be lit in honour of the Master. The rest you will see when we have completed the ritual," said Siggi, handing me the athamé.

I took the dagger and stood next to the baby. I wished I could control myself, but a dark and invisible force guided me along.

"Do it! Do it!" The adepts shouted in unison, urging me to perform that act of great wickedness.

"Valentino, you too will benefit from the Master's gifts. Don't hesitate, do it now!" Father Ramón said in a low and persuasive tone.

But something unexpected happened. Snorri had come to my rescue.

"The ritual will not be done this time. The Hidden People no longer want to be your accomplice," announced the elf.

Then Snorri grabbed the dagger and, without hesitation, threw it against the wall of the crypt.

"How dare you? You are a creature of the Master. You should not have interfered. Now you will pay the consequences," said Father Ramón angrily.

Logi took back the dagger and struck the poor elf several times in the chest, who fell examining the ground.

"Evil always triumphs, it is inevitable. Take the dagger and conclude the ritual," said Siggi who in the meantime had cleaned the blade of the athamé with a linen cloth.

I did what I had to do to get rid of the evil effects of the diabolical miracle. Unfortunately, I had no other choice. I grabbed the dagger and sank the blow. Immediately after having accomplished that wickedness, which would have marked me for the rest of my life, I turned and walked in tears towards the exit of that hell. So I left that mess behind. Those subhuman beings would no longer torment me. I was free now, but at what cost?

10 ON THE WAY TO THE LIGHT

Eighteen months had passed since that cursed day; eighteen months, like the eighteen runes used for the success of a diabolical miracle. After those sad events, my life changed drastically and went into crisis. Killing a newborn baby was for me an indelible mark that caused deep existential disturbances to me.

That day I instantly became like Cain the son of Adam who had killed his brother Abel, and just like him I felt "more cursed than the earth who had opened his mouth to receive the blood of that innocent from my hand." How could I have obtained from God the redemption for the sin I had committed? Although the sorcerers, or rather the king-priests had tried in every way to reward me for helping them complete the ritual, I returned all their "gifts" to the sender. These "gifts" consisted of prestigious job offers, winnings in lotteries in which I had never participated, and even marriage proposals from beautiful women. I recognized those cursed gifts and I refused them; for this reason, I was forced to reluctantly leave my Iceland, the island that had welcomed me warmly. I had no other choice. I gave up my career as a professor and I decided to go back to Naples, waiting for better days. My father Antonio and my mother Anna never knew anything about what happened that night in the crypt of the cathedral.

I would have liked, however, to confide in my friend Marco, but I was not allowed to. The sect prevented me from meeting him and even sending him letters. Marco was sentenced to sixteen years in prison, the maximum sentence under Icelandic law for murder offenses. Then I took refuge in prayer, trying to ease my pain. After all, I too was a murderer, but no earthly court would have tried me. I had the safe conduct of the sect. They would have obstructed any type of investigation into Vesturbær's tragic events. Exactly as I had imagined, theirs was a very powerful millennial cult, supported by corrupt and influential men. It was the sect that moved the threads behind the scenes in a world where affiliates moved free to commit any wickedness. An elite of people who had acquired great financial, political and religious influence over the centuries; profound connoisseurs of the social structures of the countries, their cultural characteristics, popular beliefs and anything else that can condition and control the fate of a nation.

Before returning to Italy, in the three days following the human sacrifice that took place in the Reykjavík catacombs, I contacted a paranormal expert, named Ragnar. I wanted to fix something before saying goodbye to my old Icelandic life. I spoke to him on the phone and told him that I needed his help.

"There is a soul that has been lost and I would like you to guide it towards the light," I explained directly.

That lost soul was not mine, but that of Gudrun. I wanted her spirit to finally find the right way back to Heaven, thus breaking the bond she had with me because of the ritual that took place 180 years earlier. The time had come to end it.

"When someone contacts me for a ghost, I put my face on it and I don't back away until I can solve the problem," said Ragnar, showing confidence in his voice.

We met at the cemetery of Hólavallagarður in front of the tomb of Gudrun. Ragnar asked me to describe her so that he could better connect spiritually with her.

"Don't be afraid. I'm here to show you the path to the light," Ragnar announced as he entered a trance.

Gudrun received the psychic's message and almost immediately appeared beside me. She was radiant and my heart was beating fast with the emotion of seeing her again, even if only for a short moment. She gave me her hand and caressed my face.

"Valentino, thanks for closing the circle. We two will love each other forever," she said candidly.

"There are good people and bad people in the realm of the dead as well as in the living. The mere fact of being dead does not make you an angel. But now the time has come to guide you to the light. Your ordeal is over. I will accompany you spiritually to the afterlife entrance. If you want to hug Valentino for the last time, do it now," Ragnar urged.

She came over and gave me a very strong hug. Then we kissed gently. They were instants of pure and passionate happiness.

"*Ciao* Gudrun."

She did not reply but looked at me with a wonderful look, full of love and resignation. The two walked along the avenue of the cemetery for a few meters. She never turned around again, but I still followed her with teary eyes. The sky was grey and the wind made itself felt aggressively. Winter was almost upon us. Suddenly I saw a glow that illuminated both. The psychic pointed a direction and Gudrun followed it naturally. Another ten seconds passed, and then she disappeared into thin air, consuming herself in a glimmer of dazzling light.

ABOUT THE AUTHOR

Valerio Gargiulo is an Italian writer of supernatural fiction and fantasy, based in Reykjavik, Iceland. He has been active both in the field of legal advice and research. He studied at Reykjavik University and finished his Master of Laws in 2015. Previously, after completing a Bachelor of Laws at the University of Naples Federico II, he has been freelancing, drafting reports and legal agreements. He also worked as a preschool teacher and EEG technologist. He's the author of The Incredible Journey of a Neapolitan Puffin and Back to Thule.

9 789935 951519